Peter Pan

Wendy, John and Michael Darling lived in London. One night, Wendy woke up to find a strange looking boy sitting on the floor, crying bitterly.

"My name is Wendy," she said. "Who are you? Why are you crying?"

"I'm Peter Pan," the boy replied. "I'm crying because my shadow won't stick to me."

"Please don't cry," Wendy said. "Let me fix it." She sewed Peter's shadow to the tip of his shoes. Peter was delighted. Wendy woke up John and Michael.

"Fly back to Neverland with me and my fairy, Tinker Bell," Peter begged. "I can teach you all how to fly. We could all live together and have fun."

"Let's all fly to Neverland," Wendy said excitedly.

The children were soon flying around the room, and then, woosh! Out of the window they all flew.

Wendy, John and Michael flew behind Peter Pan and Tinker Bell, following the golden arrows that marked the way to Neverland. Finally, they were flying over the island.

"I am the captain of the lost boys. They live with me and Tinker Bell," Peter said. "The Indians live over there, and the mermaids live in the lagoon. And there are pirates too, led by the evil Captain Hook."

"Pirates!" exclaimed Wendy, John and Michael, all in the same breath. Wendy was frightened, but Michael and John wanted to see the pirates right away.

"Hook's the meanest pirate ever," Peter warned, "but he's afraid of the crocodile. The crocodile bit off Hook's hand and liked the taste so much that it follows him, hoping for more. Luckily for Hook, the crocodile swallowed Hook's watch too. It goes 'Tick, Tock,' and warns Hook when the crocodile is nearby."

"Oh, my God!" cried Wendy, not sure if she really wanted to stay in Neverland after knowing about the pirates.

Peter led Wendy, John and Michael to his house under the woods. They entered through a door hidden in an old tree stump. When the lost boys saw Wendy, they shouted, "Hooray! Will you be our mother?"

"I'm only a little girl myself," Wendy answered. "I would not know how to take care of you all." But the lost boys looked so sad that she agreed and said, "I'll do my best."

That night Wendy tucked the boys into the bed and told them the tale of Cinderella.

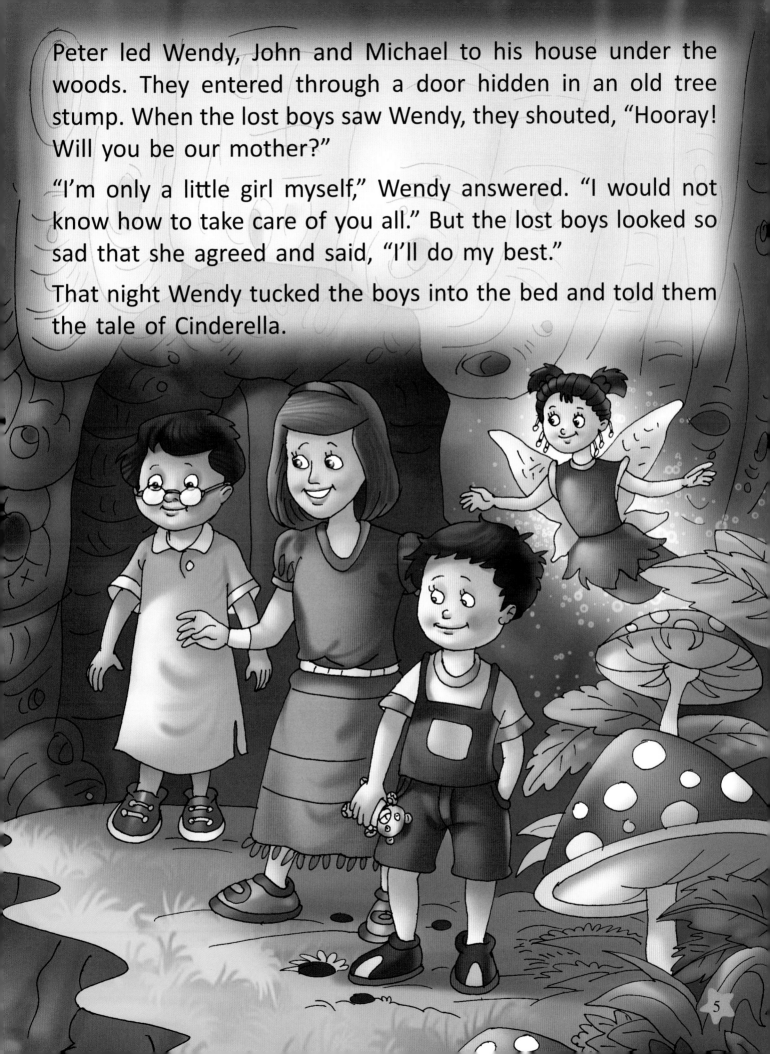

6

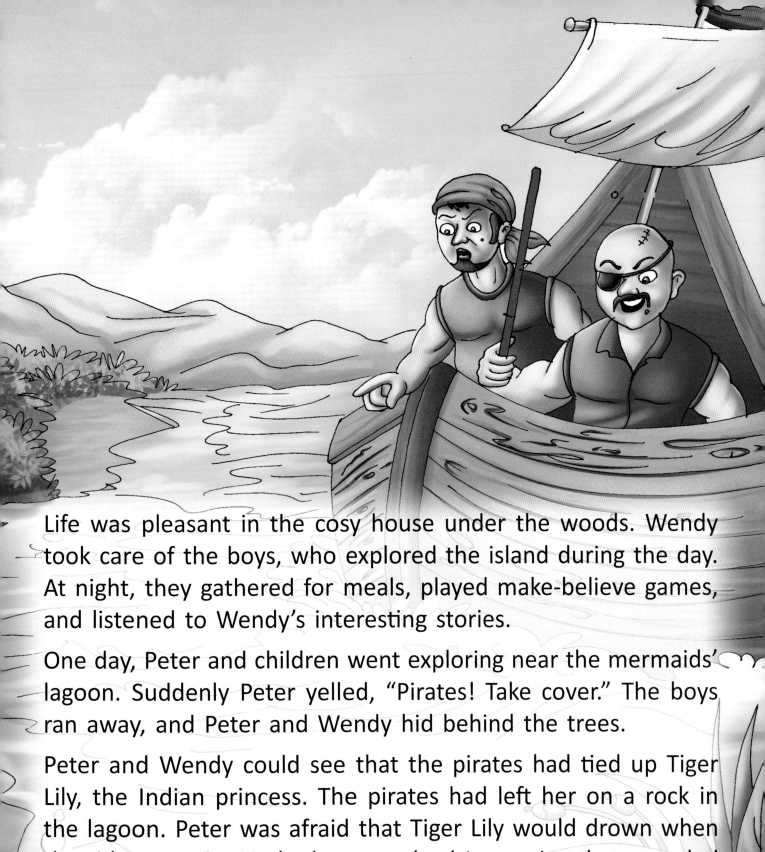

Life was pleasant in the cosy house under the woods. Wendy took care of the boys, who explored the island during the day. At night, they gathered for meals, played make-believe games, and listened to Wendy's interesting stories.

One day, Peter and children went exploring near the mermaids' lagoon. Suddenly Peter yelled, "Pirates! Take cover." The boys ran away, and Peter and Wendy hid behind the trees.

Peter and Wendy could see that the pirates had tied up Tiger Lily, the Indian princess. The pirates had left her on a rock in the lagoon. Peter was afraid that Tiger Lily would drown when the tide came in. He had to save her! In a voice that sounded just like Captain Hook's, he shouted, "Set her free!"

"But, Captain," the pirates yelled, "you ordered us to bring her here!" They looked around but could not see their captain anywhere.

"Let her go!" Peter roared, still sounding like Hook.

"Aye, aye," the pirates said, and set Tiger Lily free. She quickly swam back to the Indian camp.

When Captain Hook found out what had happened, he knew Peter had tricked his pirates. Hook was furious, very furious!

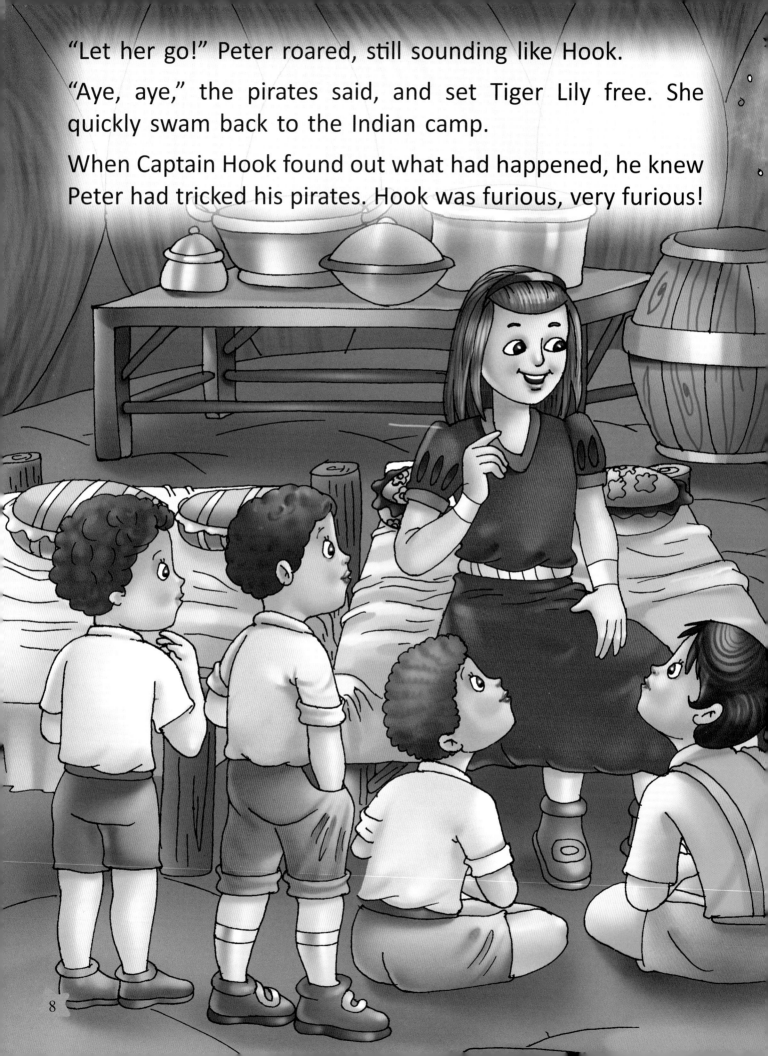

That night, Wendy told the boys a story about three children who had left their parents and flown off to Neverland. Their parents missed them very much. Though the children loved Neverland, they had never really forgotten their home.

"Did they ever go back?" the lost boys asked.

"Oh, yes," Wendy replied. "They flew home to their mummy and daddy, and everyone was happy."

The story made Wendy, John and Michael homesick. They decided to fly back home. "If you come back with us," Wendy told the lost boys, "I'm sure our parents would be happy to adopt you."

"Hooray!" shouted the boys, jumping with joy. Wendy asked Peter if he and Tinker Bell would come home with them too. But Peter didn't want to live where grown-ups would tell him what to do.

Peter was sad that his friends were leaving, but he wanted the children to reach home safely. He asked Tinker Bell to guide them on their trip back home.

Early next morning, Tinker Bell and the children left the house under the woods. But Captain Hook's pirates were hiding nearby. They captured all the children, tied them up, and marched them towards their ship.

Clever that she was, Tinker Bell escaped, and hurried back to tell Peter what had happened.

"It's Hook or me this time!" yelled Peter with anger as he and Tinker Bell flew off to save Wendy and the boys.

On the pirates' ship, Captain Hook asked, "Who wants to become a pirate?" All the boys shook their heads.

"Then make them walk the plank!" Hook roared. The boys tried to look brave, but deep inside they were afraid.

Suddenly, they heard, "Tick, Tock, Tick Tock." Now it was Captain Hook's turn to be afraid.

But it was Peter who was imitating the sound of the watch that was inside the crocodile, "Tick, Tock, Tick, Tock." He flew onto the deck and shouted, "I've got you now, Hook!"

Captain Hook jumped up and swung at Peter with his sword. Peter was quick and stepped away. He slashed at Hook with his own sword until they came close to the edge of the ship.

Peter made a lunge with his sword, and Hook fell into the sea where the crocodile was waiting for him. He gobbled up Captain Hook in one delicious bite and that was the end of Captain Hook!

With Hook gone forever, Peter and Tinker Bell set off for London with Wendy and the boys.

Wendy's parents were delighted to have their children back. They gladly agreed to adopt all the lost boys. They asked Peter too to stay with them, but Peter refused, saying, "I'm going back to stay in Neverland where I never ever have to grow up."

"Goodbye everyone," said Peter Pan as he and Tinker Bell waved them goodbye and flew back to Neverland.